Soup is running for school president. So is Norma Jean Bissell, which means poor Rob is torn between voting for his best pal Soup or for his sweetheart. A hectic campaign ensues, and the two boys paint Soup's name in large red letters on sour-faced Mr. Cyrus McGinley's barn. Then comes trouble with a goat, a ladder, and a truck tire; bruises from bully Janice Riker, iodine from Miss Boland the nurse, a love letter from Norma Jean, and sturdy words of Vermont logic from Miss Kelly.

As bright and sunny as autumn in Vermont, here's a story about kids being kids . . . with a teacher to believe in as much as she so fervently believes in them.

Books by Robert Newton Peck

Soup for President

Robert Newton Peck

ILLUSTRATED BY TED LEWIN

Alfred A. Knopf ✦ *New York*

THIS IS A BORZOI BOOK PUBLISHED BY ALFRED A. KNOPF, INC.

Text Copyright © 1978 by Robert Newton Peck
Illustrations Copyright © 1978 by Alfred A. Knopf, Inc.
All rights reserved under International and Pan-American Copyright
Conventions. Published in the United States by Alfred A. Knopf,
Inc., New York, and simultaneously in Canada by Random House
of Canada Limited, Toronto. Distributed by Random House, Inc.,
New York.
Manufactured in the United States of America 10 9 8 7 6 5 4 3 2 1

Library of Congress Cataloging in Publication Data

Peck, Robert Newton.   Soup for President
Summary: Rob manages Soup's campaign for class president in their
small Vermont town.   [1.   Friendship—Fiction]   I.   Lewin, Ted.
II.   Title.   PZ7.P339Pr   [Fic]   77–13522
ISBN 0–394–83675–8   ISBN 0–394–93675–2 lib. bdg.

To my first love,
Norma Jean Bissell—

and to my last,
Dorrie

Soup for President

1

"Hike," said Janice.

I hiked it. Wobbling in flight like a wounded goose, the lopsided football flew to our fullback, who tucked it into her arm, charging forward with her head down and her chunky legs churning.

Grunting an "oof," I tried my darndest to throw a block on Eddy Tacker who was the biggest and best tackler on the other team. Eddy's elbow introduced itself into my cheek, but I grabbed his shirttail like I was hanging on for murder. Knocked down, I still wouldn't quit. I also bit Ally Tidwell on the ankle. This may sound easy, but it really isn't. You'd have to look all over Vermont to find an ankle dirtier than Ally's.

"Get her! Get her!"

Soup was yelling, and Eddy was stomping on my ear

so that I'd turn loose my hold on his shirttail. Mud was in my left eye, but squinting, I saw Soup try to tackle Janice. It was like a kitten trying to trip a truck. Out shot her arm. Her fist met Soup's chin and over he went. This bit of stiff-arming slowed Janice down a bit, just long enough for Rolly McGraw to jump on her back and pull her hair.

"Fall down, ya!" yelled Rolly.

I hollered. "Come on, Janice!"

Even with Rolly on her back, with his hands over her eyes, Janice fumbled forward and fell *under* (not over) the goal line, which was Mrs. Tomasa's clothes rope. Many a touchdown had been scored when a ballcarrier had scooted between the wet legs of Mr. Tomasa's long red underwear.

"Touchdown!" hollered Miss Boland.

Rolly was still trying to bulldog Janice into the turf, even though a hoarse blast from Miss Boland's tarnished whistle signified that Janice had proved herself once again to be the best doggone fullback in school.

Over trotted Miss Boland to help unsnarl the tangled nest of bodies and bruises. After each play, Miss Boland (our County Nurse as well as our football coach) examined us all, the crying as well as the crippled. She dusted us off, dried our tears, and often called the next play. None of us, possibly with the exception of Janice Riker, would have learned anything about the game of football had it not been for Miss Boland. She was the only daughter in a family of eight, so what she had learned of survival, she passed along to us.

"Good run," said Miss Boland.

"Thanks," said Janice.

"My shirt's tore," said Eddy, glowering in my direction.

I countered with, "So's my ear."

"Let me look," said Miss Boland as she unraveled her hogpile of hurting athletes. My ear received attention ahead of Eddy Tacker's shirt. It really stung, and sounded like a pipe organ.

"Is it bleeding?"

"You'll endure," said Miss Boland.

"Soup's lip is all puffed up," I said.

Miss Boland inspected Soup's injury, announcing that he, too, would live to face another fullback. I was certain sure that Soup was not overly eager to try another tackle on Janice. She was just too tough to tangle with, and I always smiled whenever Janice picked me. Eddy Tacker and Janice were the usual captains. Always, I wanted to be on Janice's team. Wow, could that kid play football!

Tweet sounded Miss Boland's whistle.

"Now then," she said, "what's the score?"

"Sixty to nothing," grumbled Soup.

"That's right, Miss Boland. That last one was Janice's tenth touchdown."

"The sides ain't even," Eddy griped.

"Apparently not," said Miss Boland. "Well, you're all battered a bit, but you're playing better than you did last week."

"We are?"

"You sure are. In fact, I just might be able to dig up the scratch for a *new* football. I'll take it up with Miss Kelly."

We all cheered.

"Our old one," Miss Boland said, as she took the ball from Janice, "is just about on her last legs."

The seams had given way in several spots, the leather was dry and scuffed up, and the laces could not have handled one more knot. Rather than a football, it looked like a rotten pumpkin. Tossing the football into the air, Miss Boland caught it. Holding the football under one arm, she twirled her whistle in circles, winding and unwinding its frayed cord around her chubby index finger. Miss Boland always wore a white dress, white stockings, and white shoes. Today, she also wore her old school sweater with a big B on the back.

"My ankle hurts."

"How come?" asked Miss Boland.

"Somebody bit me," said Ally.

"Fetch it here."

Miss Boland opened her nurse's kit, displaying her impressive supply of swabs and pills and medication. I saw her chunky hand trudge along the corks until her forefinger stepped on the right bottle. Up it came.

"Iodine!" gasped Ally.

No one else said anything. We all just stared at the little bottle that contained a brown liquid that burned like a March stove. There was hardly a kid in the whole school that hadn't suffered a lick or two of Miss Boland's iodine. And it smarted like all fury.

"No," said Ally.

"You got bit, didn't you?"

"Yes'm," Ally replied to Miss Boland.

"Boy, there's nothing dirtier than the human mouth."

"Honest?"

"Honest," said Miss Boland. "So help me, I druther get snake-bit than get bit by Rob Peck."

"Me?" I asked.

"You," she said. "I saw you do it. Human mouth is full o' germs. Dirty as a hen house. You don't believe it? Well, let's say," said Miss Boland, as she pulled the brown cork out of her iodine bottle, "that you get yourself mixed up in a fist fight."

"Then what?"

"*And* you punch some lucky fella in the teeth . . ."

"Lucky?"

"Right. Because the next day, that old fist of *yours* will rise up like Christmas baking. Big as a baseball glove. And do you know what causes it?"

"No," we all admitted.

"Spit," said Miss Boland, dunking a white swab on a stick, pulling it up brown from the bottle of iodine. "Human spit is worse'n rattlesnake venom."

"It really is?" asked Ally, his eyes were staring at the reddish-brown ball of cotton that Miss Boland held closer and closer to my teethmarks on his ankle. That iodine smelled somewhere between a horse and a hospital.

"Betcher boots."

"Iodine stings." Ally was crying.

"You want to lose your leg?"

"No'm."

"Hold him still."

Soup grabbed one arm and I grabbed the other while Janice grabbed Ally around the neck.

"I didn't say throttle him. Let loose. Ally, stretch forward that chawed-up shank of yours and yell *yahoo*."

"Yell it loud?"

"Loud as you can."

"*Yahoo*," yelled Ally.

"Pinch him," said Miss Boland.

It was sort of fun; except for Ally, who was dancing around a bit with a brown cloud of iodine fixed to his ankle. Sure was amusing. Ally Tidwell was crying and we were all laughing, even though my stomach had a nag inside it because of the fact that Ally's getting toothbit was all *my* fault.

"Don't be a baby," I told Ally.

"It stings."

"Rob . . ."

I turned to look at Miss Boland.

"No, don't look at me. Look at Ally," she said.

"What for?"

"Your ear's cut worse'n I figured."

Oh, *no*, I thought. Not the iodine.

"No, it isn't," I said.

Miss Boland said it was. So did good old Soup. And then, so did Janice. That's the trouble with fullbacks. They never appreciate centers.

"Best I put something on it."

"Like what?"

"Iodine," whispered Soup.

"I'm sorry I bit you, Ally," I said.

"What about my shirt?" asked Eddy Tacker.

"Put iodine on it," said Soup. The kids laughed. All except me. I was too busy looking at the fresh swab that Miss Boland withdrew from what she always called her "bundle of arrows." Then she dipped the arrow in poison.

"Step close, Rob."

"I don't want to."

"Do you want your ear to fall off?"

"No'm, I don't."

"Fraidy cat," said Soup.

Behind my eyes, I could feel the tears starting to form. Gee, I sure didn't want to cry. Not over a little old swipe of dumb iodine.

"Do you want to yell *yahoo?*"

"Not very much."

"It'll help." Miss Boland smiled.

I turned to Ally. "Does it help?"

"Not a whole darn lot." Ally scowled at the nurse.

"Ya see?" I said to Miss Boland. "It doesn't help."

"It doesn't hurt."

"You mean the iodine?"

"Oh, that may tingle a mite. Just enough to let you know that it'll kick the stuffing out of the infection. You don't want a pair of germs nesting in your ear, do you, and raising up a ruckus?"

"No," I said, "I don't guess I do."

"Pinch him," said Miss Boland.

Everyone laughed and pinched, Janice especially hard, and I yelled, "Yahoo! Yahoo!" about as loud as anybody ever yelled it. Everybody in Vermont heard it, and maybe some of the crosslake Yorkers. They heard it in Boston and they heard it in Ohio and even out in Tulsa.

Ally was right. It doesn't help. The doggone iodine hurt like all get-up-crazy. I could swear that Miss Boland tied a hornet to my ear. If it hurt *me* this much, I started to feel sorry for those poor little germs. But then it smarted less and less, and Miss Boland put a football bandage on my ear and on Ally's ankle and sewed up Eddy's shirt. She sure knew a whole lot about being a good County Nurse.

I liked Miss Boland best when she sewed up the football.

2

"Now," ordered Miss Kelly.

"But we didn't mean it," said Soup.

"Perhaps not," Miss Kelly said in her patient voice, a sound which held neither joy nor anger, "but *I* mean it. Luther, you and Robert will not sit together for the rest of the day."

"We're real sorry, Miss Kelly," I said, as I got to my feet beside the double desk. Bending over, I picked up the red can-rubber that Soup had so expertly used to snap my sore ear with. It still smarted.

Soup didn't budge.

Instead, his eyes stayed fixed on Miss Kelly's right hand, the one that Soup called "her gun hand." Our teacher possessed the fastest right east of Lake Champlain and west of New Hampshire. Not one single cowboy in all the Saturday movies that were ever cranked (not even Buck Jones or Tom Mix) whipped a faster draw with a Colt .44 six-shooter than Miss Kelly could muster with her ruler. *And then, there it was!* Up and leveled at Soup and me, twelve mean inches of heartless hickory with an edge of cold steel, held in her steady and able fingers.

I heard Soup swallow.

Soup and I separated quickly, as Miss Kelly's weapon had a long range of uses, disciplinary as well as geographical. Her ruler could point out Ethiopia with the same facility that it helped maintain the high standards of schoolroom conduct. Soup then sat with Ally and I remained alone. Order restored, Miss Kelly's ruler returned to its holster, the center drawer of her desk.

"What year are we in?" asked Miss Kelly.

The heavenly hand of Norma Jean Bissell took flight, a blend of grace and scholarship. "It's 1936," she said, as I listened to her recitation with unwavering devotion. She wasn't like other girls. She was . . . Norma Jean Bissell.

"Yes," agreed Miss Kelly. "It is September, 1936. Who can tell us what event to expect this coming November?"

Janice Riker's face suddenly brightened with a rare burst of insight. "I know," she said. "Pa said our cow's to freshen."

Miss Kelly sighed. No one heard her sigh, but I saw her do it, because it was what Miss Kelly always did following a recitation by Janice Riker. It sort of made me laugh. A big mistake! Janice caught me smiling and held up her knuckles. Janice had fists the size of cannonballs, and both were twice as hard. As my hand shot up to cover my grin, I knew for sure and certain that I was in for it and that Janice Riker would get me after school.

"Congratulations," said Miss Kelly. "A new calf is always welcome. However, the event that I have in mind is one of a political nature."

"Like voting," said Soup.

"*Yes*," said Miss Kelly. "And what is going to happen in November?"

"I know," I said. "Everybody all over the town knows. Alf Landon is going to whup the tar out of that Democrat."

As I saw Miss Kelly's eyebrows lift slightly, I began to wonder what I'd said wrong. Then it sort of hit me. I'd said a *dirty word!* Democrat.

"Gee," I said quickly, "I didn't mean to say that word. It just sort of slipped out."

As I apologized, my eyes couldn't help wandering over to the washstand in the corner upon which rested, in its usual puddle of yellow goo, the big brown bar of laundry soap. The bar of Octagon served a dual purpose; cleansing hands and foul mouths, the latter function supervised personally by Miss Kelly's insistence on clean language.

"I won't ever say that word again."

"Which word, Robert?"

As Miss Kelly asked the question, I saw the smile lift her chin. Even though she had gray hair and was near to a hundred years old, there wasn't one doggone soul in all of Vermont who could smile the way our teacher smiled. When her face was happy, she could sugar you like a doughnut. And right now, she was trying not to smile, even though she knew that all over town, most folks agreed that Democrat was a dirty word.

Again I looked at the soap.

"Despite the fact," said Miss Kelly, as she sort of sank weakly into her chair, "that many of us in town are Republicans, I believe we can speak of both parties, Democrat *and* Republican, without further fear of embarrassment."

It was my turn to sigh.

"Robert, you may put your hand down. And to resume, in November your mothers and fathers will vote to elect a *new* president."

Miss Kelly was a solid Republican.

"Who," asked Miss Kelly, "can name one of our great presidents of the United States?"

"George Washington," we all said.

"Abraham Lincoln," we all said.

"And . . ." waited Miss Kelly.

"Calvin Coolidge," we all said.

"*Yes*," nodded Miss Kelly, "as Calvin Coolidge was the only president to ever come from . . ."

"Vermont," we all chorused.

"And where is Landon from?"

"Kansas," we said, after a quiet moment of deliberation. Janice Riker mumbled, "the Capital of England."

I wasn't quite sure where Kansas was, but I figured it was probably closer than Ethiopia. We sort of felt sorry for President Roosevelt because he had to admit he was from New York. To be injun honest about it, I really didn't know too much about President Roosevelt; except that his first name was Franklin, but I think his pals in the Rough Riders all called him Teddy.

"Thus," said Miss Kelly, "when November comes, who will elect the president?"

"People that vote," said Soup. "And they add up the votes by states, not just by the numbers and stuff."

"Very good, Luther," said Miss Kelly to Soup. "We are all pleased that you have chosen to gain our attention by achievement rather than by distraction."

Soup cracked a wide grin. He got the highest marks in the whole school; and that was some honor, seeing as there was twenty-eight of us. Soup's report card always said A, A, A, A, A in geography, spelling, reading, writing, arithmetic. But he never got an A in deportment. His pa asked him once what deportment was and Soup told him that it was playing store like in the Emporium up in Burlington. When it came to getting away with pranks and like that, Soup was a greased eel.

"The thought has occurred to me," Miss Kelly continued, "that in order to better understand our national election, we could have our very own election, right here at school."

"You mean," asked Eddy Tacker, "some of us would be Republicans and some of us Democrats?"

"Exactly," said Miss Kelly. "Edward, you have made an excellent suggestion. So, who wants to be a Republican?"

Twenty-eight hands went up.

"Who wants to be a Democrat?"

Twenty-eight hands went down.

"Hmm." Miss Kelly mused. "This poses a bit of a problem. However, I think we can resolve it if we create new names for our two parties. Let's have some suggestions."

"Elephants," I said.

"Zebras," shouted Soup.

Lions, tigers, bears, snakes, pollywogs, tadpoles, and bedbugs were also mentioned, as well as the Boston Red Sox and the New York Giants, until Miss Kelly commanded our silence. She warned us that unless we became orderly, there would be little chance of a new football.

"Ah," she said, "I have it. We have fourteen boys and fourteen girls. Boys, you may all leave the room to return in five minutes, and you will decide on a name for your party and select one of you to run for school president. The girls will remain inside and do likewise while I wrestle with the window."

Out into the September afternoon we tumbled, fourteen boys, from first grade through sixth, all of us eager to be president. Eddy Tacker nominated himself, but seeing as he had to stand up against Soup and me and Rolly, he didn't have a prayer. Eddy Tacker was the second toughest kid in school. Nobody, not even Eddy, was tougher than Janice. We held a convention, consisting of Soup's sitting on Eddy's head while Rolly McGraw and I tied a few knots in his fingers. A defeat like this can ruin a political career and the upshot of our deliberations was that Soup would run for president on the boy's ticket.

We'd call ourselves the Apes.

"Miss Kelly," yelled Soup. "We're all ready to come back inside."

"Do you have a candidate?" she called, leaning from the window.

"No," I said. "All we got is Soup."

As she looked at the dust on Eddy Tacker's shirtfront with a practiced eye, I figured Miss Kelly was about to comment about the grime of the political arena, but she held off.

"Are the girls ready yet?" asked Soup.

"No," Miss Kelly answered. "They can't seem to agree."

"On what?"

"The girls have no candidate as yet." Miss Kelly came outside.

"It isn't going to be Janice, is it?" I asked, a bit apprehensive.

Miss Kelly cleared her throat. "It will be *anyone* chosen by their party. The candidate and the party name will be entirely *their* decision, and not mine."

Wetting her hanky with her tongue, Miss Kelly removed a smudge of dirt from beneath Eddy Tacker's ear. Soup was smiling, a gesture Miss Kelly chose to ignore.

"Thank you, Miss Kelly," said Eddy.

"You're quite welcome, Edward."

I never could figure out how somebody as smart as Miss Kelly could like people such as Eddy Tacker or Janice Riker. Maybe that was why she was such a good teacher. But I knew that of all the kids in the whole darn school, Miss Kelly liked *me* the best. On that I would bet every penny I had in the bank. Fourteen cents.

Girls were screaming.

"Darn you, Janice," somebody yelled.

A shoe came flying out of the school window, followed by its mate, and then by several girlish faces. The errant shoes were retrieved, order restored, and parliamentary process was once again underway. We boys went back inside.

"Have you girls made up your minds?" Miss Kelly asked, when every fidgeting body was again wedged between desk and bench.

"Yes," the girls shrieked.

Rolly McGraw announced, at Miss Kelly's request, that Soup would run for president and represent the Apes. We (all the boys) thumped our chests and grunted to signify tribal unity. Even with no fast draw of her ruler, Miss Kelly asked for order. Quietly we heard Miss Kelly ask Janice to stand up and make the opposing political announcement. Janice looked like she wanted to kick somebody with her red hightop sneakers.

"And the name of *your* party?" asked our teacher.

Janice said, "We're the Amazons."

"Dumb name," whispered Soup, even though Miss Kelly herself had been reading aloud about the Amazon women and what brave warriors they were. I think they fought to see who'd get Brazil.

"Who is your candidate?" Miss Kelly asked Janice.

"Norma Jean Bissell."

My heart sank.

3

"Higher," said Soup.

"This is as high as I can reach," I yelled over my shoulder, down to Soup who was behind me, and below, standing safely on the ground in McGinley's orchard.

"One more inch," Soup suggested.

"I'll fall off the ladder," I shouted. Already I was up on my tiptoes, my sneakers poised dead center on the very top rung. Against my hands and face, I felt the rough gray splinters of the side of Cyrus McGinley's cow barn.

"Well," said Soup, "it won't look right unless you sort of get it centered."

"If I tumble off this cussed ladder, *I* won't look so hot either."

"You want to be my campaign manager, don't you?"

"Yes," I said. What I really wanted to do was to get down off the ladder.

"So, that's what campaign managers *do*. They paint the candidate's name on the side of a barn."

"You mean like MAIL POUCH?" I asked.

"Sort of. But I ain't a chaw of tobacco."

"Nobody said you were."

"Make a mark," yelled Soup, hands cupped to his mouth, "right up where your left hand is."

"Why?"

"Because that's where the S in Soup ought to start."

"Are you sure we have enough paint?"

"It's only four letters," said Soup.

"I can spell."

"Did you mark the spot?"

"Yes," I said, not quite daring to look up at the white scribble of chalk that I had added to Mr. Cyrus McGinley's property.

"Okay," said Soup, "now reach up with your right hand and mark it, so you'll know how wide to make the top of the S."

Eyes closed, I chalked another squiggle.

"That's good enough."

"Soup . . ."

"Yeah?"

"I'm not sure that painting your name on Mr. McGinley's barn is such a hotdog of an idea."

"Why not? It pays to advertise."

"Well, because I don't think it'll help you win.'

"You're not supposed to think."

"What *am* I supposed to do?"

"Paint."

"Your uncle is going to get sore, Soup."

"Nah. Uncle Charlie is a regular guy."

Soup was busy with a large screwdriver and a chisel. Sitting on the apple-strewn ground, he began to pry up the lid from a gallon of red paint that he'd "borrowed" from his uncle's tool shed earlier that morning.

"Ya know, Rob, that S ought to be bigger."

"I want to get down."

"You just got up there."

"I still want to climb down off this ladder."

"You're not up very high. It's only a twenty-footer."

"Maybe it doesn't look so high from down where you are. From up here, it looks like one heck of a drop."

"You'll get used to it."

"What's underneath me?" I asked Soup.

"Something soft."

"Like what?"

"Manure."

"Oh, no! If I fall myself off this dumb ladder and land in a manure pile, Mama will kill me. And if *she* doesn't, Aunt Carrie will."

"They won't kill you."

"How come?"

Soup laughed. "The *fall* will."

"Some friend *you* are."

"Rob, if *you* were the candidate, I'd buy an airplane and skywrite your name as big as Vermont."

"You honest would?"

"Darn tootin'."

"How high am I?"

"More than twenty feet. It looks higher than it is."

"I want to climb down, Soup."

"Not now. Here comes the paint."

"Did the lid come off?"

"Yup."

"Is it really red?"

"Redder than the devil's longies."

As the ladder suddenly tilted, I felt gray splinters dig into the palms of my hands. Breakfast came up into my throat—outmeal, apple pie, orange juice, and a banana. The chalk slipped and joined the manure.

"For golly sake, Soup, *don't* make me laugh. I'll fall and break my butt."

"Steady now. Here I come." Soup's voice was dead serious as he started up the ladder. I didn't want to look down. Up through my sneakers, I felt his painful progress, rung by rung. One . . . two . . . three . . . I counted each jiggle of the ladder, my eyes closed tightly.

"Hurry up, Soup."

"Zgtmnpx."

Looking down, I saw at once why Soup's last remark had been so garbled. His mouth carried the paintbrush. I wanted to ask Soup right then and there why he didn't bring *two* paintbrushes, seeing as there were two of us. But then, knowing Luther Wesley Vinson as I did, it would have been a needless question. Soup was a planner. I was a painter.

"Here," said Soup.

"What?"

"Take the brush."

"Where is it?" I asked.

"Open your eyes and look."

There was Soup, handing me a paintbrush with one hand, a gallon of red paint with the other. Slowly, I bent down and took the brush.

"Now," said Soup, "take the paint."

"I can't."

"Why can't you?"

"I'll fall. We'll *both* fall."

Soup was silent for a minute, contemplating, no doubt, that *he* would also go tumbling down. I could read the deep thinking on his worried face.

"Tell ya what," said Soup.

"What?"

"Maybe I'll get Ally or Rolly to be my manager."

"You picked *me*."

"So I did. But you don't like painting," said Soup.

"Painting's okay. What I hate is *falling*."

"How do you know you hate falling? You haven't fell down yet."

"Some things in this world you don't have to actually *do* to know you don't cotton to'em. I just didn't realize it."

"Realize what?"

"That there was so much paint in politics."

"Here. Take the gallon."

"But I already got the brush. Say! You hold the paint can steady, I'll dip the brush in and paint," I told Soup.

"Somebody ought to be on the ground to check the shape of the letters."

It was useless to ask Soup which one of us would be up on the ladder painting. I don't know why I even bothered to ask: "Why do *you* get to be on the ground?"

"Because I'm closer," said Soup.

In my right hand was the brush, while the half-ring wire handle of the heavy paintcan cut into the fingers of my left. My cheek was pressed against the exterior gray timbers of Mr. Cyrus McGinley's barn. Eyes closed, I felt my sneakers on the tip-top rung, counting Soup's downward retreat.

"Okay," said Soup, "start painting."

"I might fall."

"You're not afraid, are you?"

"Not exactly."

"Then paint a big S."

Slowly, painfully, I twisted my body, my sneakers pivoting perilously on the ladder's top rung with nothing to hold onto except a brush and a gallon of very red paint. In my brain, I pictured the very red face of Mr. Cyrus McGinley, as he was telling my mother how I had defaced his barn. Then I imagined my very red behind.

"Leave a margin," said Soup.

With great care, I dipped the brush into the paint, withdrawing the bloody bristles. It sure was runny paint. Maybe I'd put too much on. Upward went my hand, higher, until red paint ran down the handle of the brush, along my wrist and up my arm. Or down my arm, headed toward my shoulder. I made the top of the S.

"It's running," said Soup.

"You don't have to tell *me*."

"Make it thicker."

"The *paint?*"

"No, the S."

I made it thicker. Down inside the sleeve of my raised arm, a small pond of red paint had started to form in my armpit. Wow, that paint was sure drippy! A drop fell from my busy brush, narrowly missing my eye. The red drip ran down along the bridge of my nose, and when I raised my chin again to look up, the drop scooted into my nostril. We moved the ladder and I started up again. When I start a job I always finish it. Paint sloshed over my sneaker.

"Soup . . ."

"Yeah?"

"Did you stir the paint?"

"Of course."

"When?"

"Well, I sort of shook it up."

"That's why it's so doggone runny. We didn't stir the paint. All the thicky gook is in the bottom of the can."

"Stir it now," said Soup.

"With what?"

"Dip the brush in deeper."

Somehow, but how I'll never really know, I painted the big runny-red S on the outside of Mr. McGinley's haybarn. My fingers cramped a bit, so I switched hands with brush and paintcan, applying the color with my left. This is harder than it sounds. Even with my right hand I'm no sign painter. Using my left, I'm a full-fledged slob. All I did was complete the O and turn my left armpit into a red puddle. Inside my shirt, paint oozed down my ribs in the direction of my bellybutton.

"Make the U smaller," said Soup.

"How come?"

We had moved the ladder again and I had already started to form the U, as Soup made his suggestion. Well, maybe good old Soup had a point. Back where he was sitting on the ground, leaning against a tree in the shade and eating an apple, he could probably see better than I could. Earlier, I had a hunch we were leaving a mite too generous a margin to the left of the S.

"We might not have enough room for the P."

"Okay," I said.

But as things worked out the U was fatter than either

the S or the O. Paint was smarting in my left eye, causing me to squint upward as I splashed and splotched my
way across Mr. McGinley's barn. This, I promised myself, would be the last time I'd ever be a campaign manager. I wondered what Norma Jean Bissell was doing to
put *her* name before the public eye. So help me, I
promised, if Soup says one word about this paint job,
I'd paint *him* red and then vote for Norma Jean.

"You're bending the P around the corner."

"I know," I told Soup, as I watched a drop of red
paint trickle down the leg of the ladder.

"Why?"

"Because we either run part of the P around the corner," I explained to my candidate, "or we nominate *you*
to ask Mr. Cyrus McGinley if he'd make his barn a bit
longer."

"It looks like SOUF," said Soup.

I was getting to the point of not caring if I'd spelled
SOUP or SOUF. Paint had passed under my belt (inside my shirt) in several spots, running little red rivulets
down into my undershorts. I almost completed the P
and then painfully climbed down the ladder, as the
gallon of paint was no longer in the can. Some of it
was barnside. Most of it was on me, dripping down my
legs, over my socks and sneakers. My arms ached.

"Good job, Rob," said Soup. "Have an apple."

We both tried to pry my red fingers off the handle of
the red brush. Cramped, they wouldn't turn it loose.
Head to toe, my clothes were stuck to my body by layers

of red paint. The ladder was red, too. And even the manure.

"Thank heaven," I said, falling to the ground in an exhausted heap, "that I didn't have to paint NORMA JEAN BISSELL."

"Yeah," agreed Soup, "with a name like that, you'da painted yourself clear out of town."

4

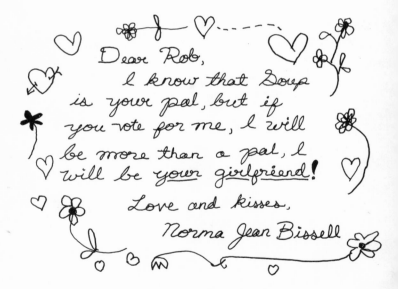

Dear Rob,

I know that Soup is your pal, but if you vote for me, I will be more than a pal, I will be your girlfriend!

Love and kisses,

Norma Jean Bissell

Over and over, I read her note, folding and stuffing it back into its pink envelope. Boy, it really smelled pretty as spring. Then I unfolded her note to read it just once more. Somewhere, far away in a distant land, I could hear Miss Kelly's voice saying something about Tibet. The notepaper was white and Norma Jean had written in pink ink. And the smell! Along the border, she had drawn little garlands of flowers and chubby pink hearts. One pink heart was fatter than the rest and looked like a tiny person with no clothes on, bending over.

"Let me see," whispered Soup.

"No," I said.

"It's from Norma Jean, isn't it?"

"None of your beeswax."

"Pals are supposed to share things."

True enough, I was thinking. But not in a million years would I ever dream of sharing somebody like Norma Jean Bissell with somebody like Soup. Maybe today would be the day that, for the very first time of my life, I would walk home with Norma Jean. And carry her books. Perhaps we'd stop on the little bridge that spans Putt's Crick and toss pebbles down into the water. Or make wishes. That was one of the places in town that sweethearts were supposed to stop. There, and under the big elm tree in the bend in the road.

"What are you thinking about?" Soup whispered.

"Nothing," I lied.

What occupied my thoughts at that very moment was a vision of my jackknife, carving a heart into the bark of the old elm. Inside the heart would be initials: RNP loves NJB.

"Are you going to let me read her note?"

"Not in a million years," I told Soup.

"How come?"

"Because it's personal."

"I bet it's a love letter," sang Soup.

"Wrong," I said. "It's about politics."

Miss Kelly kept talking about Tibet as though it were the greatest place in the whole wide world. I didn't want to be in Tibet. I wanted to be under the elm tree, after school, with Norma Jean Bissell. Eyes closed, my lips would pounce upon her freckled cheek, nibbling fairer delights than Tibet could begin to offer.

Soup giggled.

He could not have picked a poorer time; because as he sort of snickered, I was unfolding Norma Jean's note again to read it for the thirty-third time. Eyes closed, I smelled it. Ahhhh!

"Robert!"

"Yes, Miss Kelly."

"All of us in the room are reading our geography books. What are *you* reading?" Her voice was cool and stronger than a railroad spike.

"Uh . . . about Tibet."

"Perhaps, seeing as you read so much about it, you would honor us by telling us where Tibet is located?"

"Africa?"

Miss Kelly said nothing.

"South America?"

"I have asked you before," said Miss Kelly, "*not to

pass notes to each other during classroom hours."

"Yes, Miss Kelly."

"Is that a note in your hand?"

"No'm. It's a letter."

"Stand up, Robert."

"Yes'm." I stood up, causing the wooden bench to creak out a laugh at my departure. I held the note behind my back.

"Come forward, please."

I came forward.

"You may face the class and read aloud the note."

"Do I *have* to?"

"Please do."

As I looked at Norma Jean Bissell, I saw her cheeks begin to redden, and her mouth open as though she was about to scream "Stop!" Shaking her head, her eyes pleaded with mine, begging me not to read what was written in pink and festooned with happy hearts.

I will protect you, Norma Jean. There I was, a silvery knight like Ivanhoe, defending my lady fair. Would I betray her, dragging the name of Norma Jean Bissell down with me? How could my lips be sealed?

"You may read, Robert."

"Now?"

"Right now," said Miss Kelly.

"Dear Rob," I read, the letter fluttering in my hands. I cleared the frog from my throat. "I know Soup is your best friend."

"That's all?" asked Miss Kelly.

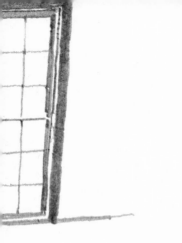

"Practically," I said. "There's a few private words that I hope you won't ask me to read."

"Rob, what's on your hands? They're *red*."

"Just some paint, Miss Kelly. Or maybe some pink ink."

"I see. You may continue."

"You mean . . . read it *all?*"

"Every word."

Oh, no! Norma Jean Bissell's face was growing redder and redder. Mine felt hotter and hotter. Again I tried to clear my throat. I didn't want to stand up front any longer. What I really wanted to do most of all was go to the bathroom. My eyes wouldn't seem to focus on the letter. Everything blurred.

"Dear Rob," I said again.

"You already did that part," said Janice.

I had the feeling behind my eyes that they were going to overflow, like a pair of stopped-up toilets.

"Dear Rob . . ."

"I'll *hate* you," whispered Norma Jean Bissell. Not

aloud, but she said it with her lips so that I could understand. But I knew it was one of those things that you sometimes say and don't mean.

"Read it," hooted Janice.

"Yeah," said Eddy.

"Louder," said Soup.

Miss Kelly softly tapped the edge of her desk with her finger and silence was restored. Only the clock was heard, as if tolling away the seconds until my doom, my punishment.

"Robert?"

"Yes, Miss Kelly."

"Please hand me the note. I may read it aloud myself."

"I . . . you can't."

She held out her hand, and I complied. As the class was silent, Miss Kelly read the note silently, only to herself. I could see she was trying not to smile.

"Robert, you may have your choice. Read the note aloud or three whacks with the ruler."

"The ruler," I said hoarsely.

Whack! Whack! *Whack!* The third one was a real lulu and it hurt like all heck. I didn't cry. But my eyes watered a bit and I was damp in a few other places. Walking back to my bench, even though my eyes were all fuzzy, I noticed Norma Jean's smile. I had held her banner high.

"Women," said Soup, "are nothing but trouble."

The note had been returned to me and was stuffed

deep into the hip pocket of my corduroys. There was nothing to do with my smarting hand except hold the edges of my geography book, read about Tibet, and wish that I could turn around to look at Norma Jean Bissell. I didn't have to wonder if she was looking at me. Now that I was her hero.

"And so," said Miss Kelly, "we see why Tibet is referred to by geographers as the Switzerland of Asia, nestled as it is, isolated in the clouds between China and India."

Outside, a car honked.

We all knew who it was. There was only one car in the county with a horn like that, making a noise that sounded like a sick chicken. Miss Kelly knew, too. In fact, she stopped talking about Tibet. Her eyes darted toward the south window and squinted the way she always did when a ruckus was happening outside the schoolhouse.

"Here she comes," said Miss Kelly.

In less than half a minute, Miss Boland, our jolly white giant of county health, burst through the door. As she stood for a second in the doorway, it seemed as though the door was still closed. Miss Boland was the size person who really knew how to fill up space. In she tromped, white shoes, white stockings, white dress and white hat, and a pink face that seemed much too eager to withhold information.

"Do we get it?" asked Miss Kelly.

Saying nothing, Miss Boland held up two chubby

fingers, suddenly crossing them as much as their bulk would allow. Her mouth widened into a promising grin.

"In the bag," she said.

We all cheered.

"Hold on," warned Miss Boland, not permitting our enthusiasm to match hers, "we don't have it yet."

"Just what did they say?" asked Miss Kelly.

"Let me sit down and take a breather. These shoes are *killing* me. I tracked down every member of the School Board, except one. And it looks good."

"Did you show them the old one?"

"Sure did," said Miss Boland.

"Good," said Miss Kelly.

"People in town musta thought I was crazier than a bedbug at Niagara Falls. Here I was, running up and down Main Street and toting that old football."

"I hope they saw that old pelter," said Miss Kelly, "and examined it enough to see that it's on its last legs."

"So am I," sighed Miss Boland, sinking into Miss Kelly's chair and loosening the laces of one of her white shoes.

"And you saw all of them."

"Almost," said Miss Boland. "I saw seven out of eight."

"What did you tell them?"

"Well, I said . . . look! You can't expect our kids to learn to play football with a pumpkin like this. We need a new ball and six boards. Or six poles."

"In my opinion," said Miss Kelly, "the boards will be

far easier to obtain than trying to pry the five dollars out of the school budget for a new ball."

Miss Boland nodded. "We can fandangle the six used boards out of Ross Drinkwine."

"For full price?"

"Half," said Miss Boland. "And the work we can do ourselves. Doesn't take much to dig four holes."

"And we'll have an *H* at both ends of the playground."

"Both ends," said Miss Boland. "Ya know, we had a pair of goalposts once. I wonder what happened to them. Small matter. We'll have ourselves a new football field *and* a new ball."

"I think we all owe Miss Boland a big thank-you for going to bat for all of us with the School Board members," said Miss Kelly.

Again, we all cheered.

"By the way, which member did you *not* see?"

"The man that really counts. Cyrus McGinley."

5

"Think," said Soup.

"I'm thinking."

"But I don't mean about Norma Jean Bissell. I mean think of a way we can make some campaign posters when we don't have any money."

"I *am* thinking."

"About what?" Soup asked me.

"Sort of about Mr. Cyrus McGinley."

"Oh, about *him*."

"If he ever finds out that you and I painted SOUP on his barn last Saturday, it'll be heck to pay. He'll report the whole thing to Sheriff Wilk."

"And we'll be wanted men," laughed Soup.

"Criminals," I sighed.

"We'll get throwed in the clink."

"Want another gumdrop?" I asked Soup.

"I s'pose *you* ate all the red ones."

"How come you're so fussy?"

"I just like red," said Soup.

"Not me," I said, "after last Saturday morning, I never want to look at anything *red* for the rest of my living days. And that includes Santa Claus."

Soup and I sat on the one-step-high porch of the candy store and finished the bag of gumdrops. You don't get a whole lot of gumdrops for a nickel. Not from old Mr. Jubert.

"Maybe *you* could get a job," Soup suggested.

"Doing what?"

"I haven't thought that out yet," said Soup, a bulge in his cheek that betrayed how he was savoring the last red gumdrop. There were tiny grains of white sugar in the bottom of the white paper bag. They rattled. Pouring them out into my hand, I gave half to Soup and ate the rest. Then we took turns smelling the bag.

"Any more ideas?"

"Yup," said Soup. "Let's sort of sidewind down the street and check out the Republican Headquarters. We can get a Landon button for our shirts."

"We each got a Landon button *yesterday*."

"I know. It's just something to do."

"Let's not waste *another* Saturday," I said, peeling a flake of red off the rim of my thumb.

"What do *you* wanna do?" Soup asked.

"Anything that doesn't take paint."

"Okay, let's go."

A few buildings away, the Vermont Republican Headquarters already had opened its doors. Everywhere you looked, there was a picture of Landon or Knox, smiling as if they already knew that the 1936 election was in the bag and poor old President Roosevelt didn't have a doggone prayer of being reelected. The headquarters was an empty store. Inside we marched, where Mrs.

Yost pinned a Landon button on Soup and then another on me. On the walls, besides Landon and Knox, were smaller pictures of the lesser candidates that were intent on capturing (or retaining) lesser offices.

One banner pleaded: *Let's Keep* KAPUSO.

"You can keep him," sneered Soup, nudging me in the ribs so that his knee-slapper didn't escape me. It didn't.

"Soup, you're a card. Come on, let's go across the street and watch Mr. Petty cut hair."

Soup's eyes suddenly grew wider.

"Cut," he said, snapping his fingers.

"Huh?"

"Rob, can't you *see?*"

"See what?"

"Let's keep Kapuso," said Soup.

"Keep him in what? A cage?"

"Look, Rob, look! All we do is *cut*. We cut off the *K* and the *A*, and lo! See what we got left."

"PUSO?"

"Mrs. Yost." Soup turned to the lady. "Rob and I want to thank you for the Landon buttons."

"Why, you're quite welcome, Luther."

"Do you know what Mr. Kapuso's running for?"

"Tax collector," said Mrs. Yost.

"Could you give us some of his banners? My folks said that it was very important to have a Republican tax collector."

"It surely is."

Laden with bundles and bunting and leaflets that im-
plored local voters to keep Kapuso collecting their taxes,
Soup and I staggered out of the Republican Headquarters heading around back, behind the Dime Emporium.
We dropped our political loot in a heap.

"What do we do now?" I asked.

"Cut," said Soup. "Throw away the K and the A of
Kapuso, then remix the four letters we got left, and it
spells . . ."

"SOUP," I barely breathed.

"Rob," he said, "you just might blossom out and
become a political genius."

Soup's jackknife was dull. Mine was duller. Yet we
cut and tore and rearranged letters with some paste
(borrowed from the unsuspecting Mrs. Yost) until our
sticky fingers appeared dry and cracked.

"Ya know, Soup . . ."

"Yeah?"

"There's only one thing wrong with these posters."

"I'm waiting."

"In looks, you don't favor Mr. Kapuso a whole lot."

"I don't, huh?"

"Nope. Not at all. Yuk, I got paste in my mouth. And
he has a mustache and you don't. What we need is
some hair."

"For what?"

"For your lip."

Soup nodded. "That makes sense. Unless you think
I could grow my own mustache by November."

"Well," I said, "seeing as it's already October, and your first whisker is yet to appear, I don't guess I'd plan on much of a showing by next month."

"We need hair," said Soup.

"Where'll we get it?"

Soup said, "Off a dog."

I sat down on Mr. Kapuso's face and laughed. So did Soup. And what made it funnier was when he sat in some paste and then got up, and there was Mr. Kapuso stuck to the back of Soup's pants.

"Here comes a dog," said Soup.

"After him, men!"

"Don't let him get away."

The dog, a mean old mongrel that people called Curr, had entered the alley where Soup and I had been cutting and pasting, took one look at us, and curled back his lip. Dogs are good judges of character.

"Stop him!" Soup was hollering.

"*You* stop him. It's *your* mustache."

"Don't you want me to win the election?"

"Sort of. Not enough to get dog-bit."

I grabbed hold of Curr's tail. It sure was one of the dirtiest tails I ever touched, and that included our cows, a pony, two or three goats, and even one or both of Janice Riker's pigtails. Curr had been rolling in something and it sure was fragrant . . . in a dismal sort of way. It wasn't really a smell. More like a kick in the nose. I turned his tail loose.

"You let go," Soup protested.

"Take my word for it," I said, "we'll call a better dog."

"How do you call a dog?"

"Easy," I told him, making my famous police-siren noise. Then I put my fist up near my mouth like an imaginary microphone and said: "Calling all Currs, calling all Currs."

Soup fell down laughing. The old dog was looking at us from some safe distance, deciding that we were more insane than dangerous.

"Hair," said Soup. "Where?"

"Maybe we could use fur."

"Fur?"

"Sure. Aunt Carrie has a genuine buffalo robe."

"Would she care if we cut off an inch or two?"

I thought for a moment. "She'd care."

"Then where can we find some . . ." Soup again snapped his fingers. "I got it!"

"Where?"

"Mr. Petty's."

Hurriedly, we formed our plan. As we entered the barbershop, Mr. Petty spotted us with a suspicious eye, as each of us had been in this place of business before.

"Both you boys got a quarter?"

"No," I said.

"Who's to get his hair cut?"

"Rob is," came Soup's reply.

"Huh," snorted Mr. Petty. "Don't look like you need a haircut to me."

"Just a trim over the ears," I lied.

"Still costs a quarter."

Knees quaking, I sat in the barberchair, thinking about the pockets of my trousers and how quarterless they were. Oh, well, Soup said it would work. Underneath the striped bib that Mr. Petty was tucking under my chin, my knees were really trembling. *Hurry*, my brain was yelling to Soup. *Hurry!*

"Mr. Petty?"

"You better wait outside," he told Soup.

"What I'd like to do, while I'm waiting for you to cut Rob's hair, is sweep your floor. Can I?"

"You wanna do *what?*"

"Sweep your floor, Mr. Petty . . . for *free*."

Our plan was working! Like a true Vermonter, Mr. Petty's face almost brightened at the thought of a costless bargain. "Free?"

Soup smiled. "Where's your broom?"

Mr. Petty nodded toward his closet.

It would be hard to say which moved slower, the barber shears or the broom. Soup didn't seem to hurry. Hair was all over the floor and what mattered was that we grab a few tufts and get out fast, before Mr. Petty could realize that he had *not* been robbed . . . or before he'd conclude that he had, for a lifetime, been sweeping away a fortune.

"Hurry," I said aloud, not meaning to.

"What's your rush?" asked Mr. Petty. "You want a haircut, don'tcha?"

I couldn't answer.

"Well, don'tcha?"

Behind Mr. Petty's back, Soup was down on his hands and knees, scooping up great handfuls of hair, stuffing it into his pockets.

"Enough," said Soup.

"S'matter with you?" asked Mr. Petty.

"I can't stand it," wailed Soup.

"Stand it. Stand what?"

"Why should some rich kids like him get haircuts and some other poor kids like me have to go without? It's not fair."

Mr. Petty's eyes narrowed, looking over his halfmoon glasses at Soup, studying him with complete distrust. "Are you some sort of a *nut?*"

"Yes," I said to Mr. Petty, "he's crazy. Hide anything you have around here that's sharp." I pointed at the row of scissors and razors.

"I'll put your broom back," said Soup. "Does it go in the bathroom?"

"I don't have a quarter, Mr. Petty."

"You *what?*"

"Can I sweep the floor instead?" I asked.

Hands in the air, turning around and around, Mr. Petty was trying to watch us both, as well as his cash drawer. Quickly, I tore off the striped bib. Words tumbled out of my mouth. If you're in trouble, Soup always said, talk like a machine gun. It sort of rattles the enemy.

"Mr. Petty," I said, "I don't have a quarter. *Please* don't arrest me. I don't want to grow up to be a criminal."

"Dang it," said Mr. Petty, "if you two hellions ever come in here again, you won't grow up at all."

"Good-bye, Mr. Petty," I yelled.

"Happy Easter," added Soup.

"It's October," said Mr. Petty.

6

"Hold still," I told Soup.

"Do you think it'll really work?"

"Not if you squirm all over the place."

"The hair tickles my nose," said Soup.

It was Monday morning, and we were on our way to school. We had stopped to sit on the big gray rock beside the road that was halfway down Duggan's Hill. I was trying my darndest to make the hair stick to Soup's upper lip, so his face would match Mr. Kapuso's, the man who was running for tax collector. I wondered why anybody would want to look like Mr. Kapuso, but there's no reason, quite often, for some of Soup's requests.

"Is it sticking?" asked Soup.

"Sort of."

"What do you mean . . . *sort* of?"

"Half is and half isn't."

"You mean," said Soup, "I have to walk around all day with only half a mustache?"

"I don't guess you will, on account of when Miss Kelly takes one good look at you, off comes the other half."

"We should of used paste," said Soup, "or glue."

"I couldn't find any. Good thing you had pancakes for breakfast, because the maple syrup is making your lip real sticky. But I still got my doubts that it'll work."

"Sure it'll work," said Soup. He licked his upper lip again to make sure the syrup wasn't too dry. "At breakfast, when Ma wasn't looking, I smeared extra syrup all over my lips."

I'll say this for good old Soup. He was never a doubter. Luther Wesley Vinson was a kid who knew that something *could* be done. And more, he got *me* to do it, and I generally caught most of the blame. Having a pal like Soup was a lot like going to sleep at night knowing that under your bed is a boa constrictor. You never knew when you'd be caught in the squeeze.

"It's working," I told Soup.

He smiled, and the makeshift mustache smiled with him. And I wondered if Miss Kelly would smile. Then, the more I thought about her, the more I knew she would.

Miss Kelly smiled.

Soup and I paraded into school that Monday morning, holding up a crudely cut poster of red, white, and blue, featuring the face of Mr. Kapuso, which read (in adjusted lettering), "SOUP for Tax Collector." Mr. Kapuso's mustache looked a bit more even than Soup's. It isn't easy to stick a fake mustache on a kid like Soup when all you have to work with is the half-dried remains of breakfast syrup plus some hair sweepings off Mr. Petty's floor. Few campaign managers, I told myself, could have done any better.

I didn't dare look at Norma Jean Bissell.

If I did, that funny feeling would come creeping into my stomach. Soup was my best pal. But I had to confess to myself that Norma Jean was sort of my sweetheart and that someday, if I was lucky, she would become Mrs. Robert Newton Peck. I often wondered which girl in the school would someday cast aside her name and become Mrs. Luther Wesley Vinson. In a way I sort of hoped it would be Janice Riker.

"Miss Kelly," asked Soup, "can . . . *may* we tack my poster up on the wall?"

Miss Kelly said we could. And she said that the whole situation was quite amusing. How ironic, she said, that at last a politician had put a mustache on a kid.

Soup pushed tacks into the bottom corners of the poster, the two that were easy to reach, while I finally managed to get one tack into the top. The other tack wouldn't go in.

"Push," said Soup, holding me up in the air.

"I'm pushing."

"Push a little harder," grunted Soup.

Miss Kelly brought her ruler and with one gentle but firm tap, the head of the tack flattened against Soup's poster. As we backed away from our art, I discovered that we'd pasted the S a little lower than the OU and the P a bit higher, which sort of made Soup, as well as poor Mr. Kapuso, look like a couple of crooked politicians.

"Hooray for Soup," yelled Rolly.

"Boo!" yelled Janice, standing up on her bench. "We want Bissell. Hip, hip, hooray for the Amazons! Down with the Apes."

Suddenly all the girls were chanting: "We want Bissell. We want Bissell. We want Bissell."

Norma Jean's face was turning pink, but I could see that she was happy. She was going after being president like a goose after a June bug. Everybody was cheering, even Miss Kelly, as she believed that we all have to get enthusiastic once in a while, because if we don't, we'd all become turnips.

"Is it true?" Norma Jean asked me while everyone else was shouting his head off. "Are you really Soup's campaign manager?"

"Yup," I said.

"I was hoping," she hollered into my ear, "that you'd vote for me."

"Well," I told her, "even though Soup is my best pal, I sort of want to vote for you."

"Honest?"

"Sure. By the way, who's *your* campaign manager?"

"Janice."

"Janice *Riker?*"

"She wanted the job," said Norma Jean, "so I figured that if she was half as good at politics as she was at fullback, I might stand a chance to beat Soup."

"Enough," said Miss Kelly. "All the Apes and all the Amazons will now settle down. Places, everyone."

We took our seats. Soup was ordered to remove his mustache.

"Now then," said Miss Kelly, "the election is only a few days away, as it will soon be November. And we shall all vote on the first Tuesday of the month."

"Which month?" asked Janice Riker.

"August," whispered Soup into my ear, and I was about to explode, just as Miss Kelly shot us each a warning stare.

"November." Miss Kelly sighed. "And now we shall all take out our geography books so that we may resume the study of Canada, our friendly neighbor to the north. Can anyone tell us what the climate of Canada is like?"

Soup yelled out, "Canada dry!"

Miss Kelly laughed. We all did. Then she ordered us to settle down and concentrate on Alberta and Manitoba, or there would be no football at noon recess and no election in November. So, in order not to disappoint Soup and Norma Jean as well as Mr. Roosevelt and Mr. Landon (not to mention Mr. Kapuso), we settled down to search Canada for Louise and Jasper. It was fun when we all tried to say *Bamfff*.

"I got an idea!"

We all turned to look at Janice, who didn't get too many ideas; except those relating to a football or a fist. And even Miss Kelly seemed to be curious.

"On election day," said Janice, "we ought to have a football game. Girls against boys."

"Even sides," said Eddy Tacker.

Miss Kelly, who knew more about football than she openly admitted, allowed as this might be a good idea, provided that she and Miss Boland would serve as referee and umpire. "And," added Miss Kelly, "it might just be a festive way to christen our *new* football."

"When are we getting it?" Soup asked.

"As soon," Miss Kelly explained, "as we receive a unanimous vote from the School Board."

"What does *unanimous* mean, Miss Kelly?"

"It means everyone has to be in favor of getting our school a new football, and of course the six pieces of lumber as well, so we can construct an *H* at both ends of the gridiron."

"Does that mean," I asked with my arm raised, "that Mr. Cyrus McGinley has to vote, too?"

Miss Kelly nodded.

We continued to pore over our geography books, unscrambling the mysteries of the Yukon and listening to Miss Kelly tell about how much fun the Eskimo people had building an igloo and riding in a dogsled. And eating blubber.

Always after geography came arithmetic.

"Football," said Miss Kelly, "can be very useful in learning our multiplication tables." As she spoke, our old beat-up football was under her arm. "For example, numbers are used to call signals before Rob hikes the ball to Janice. Correct?"

"*Yes*," we agreed heartily.

"So let's imagine we are to play football right here in the schoolroom. Each of you will have a turn at calling a signal. Rob, get ready to center the ball to me."

"To *you?*" I asked Miss Kelly.

"Yes, to me. Ready?"

"Ready," I said, prepared to snap the ball back between my legs to the teacher.

"Seven! Nine! Sixty-three! Hike!"

I hiked the ball and Miss Kelly caught it. "You see?" she asked us. "Seven times nine *is* sixty-three. My third number is the product of the first two. But unless my third number is correct, whoever is the center does *not* pass the football. Are there any questions?"

"No," we said, hardly able to stay seated on our benches. This was sure a lickety idea.

"Who goes first?" asked Norma Jean Bissell.

"Boys," said Soup.

"Girls," said Miss Kelly.

"Eight! Six! Forty-eight," said Sue Terwilliger, and Alice Wilson hiked the ball to her. Sue dropped it and everybody moaned.

"Good play," said Miss Kelly, "because six times eight *is* forty-eight."

We went through our multiplication tables, using the biggest numbers we knew. Ally Tidwell hiked the football too high; Soup missed it, and it knocked over our globe, but not even Miss Kelly seemed to care. I got to hike the ball to Norma Jean, and then she hiked it to Rolly McGraw. It sure was amazing how often we got the right answer. We even played the game again when we all went outdoors at noon recess.

"Six! Nine! Forty-one!" said Janice.

7

"YOU'RE in trouble."

"Me?" I asked Soup.

"I don't mean your Aunt Blooper."

We were walking home from school, kicking pebbles along the dirt road that goes by the quarry and then rounds the bend to our house. Looking past our cowbarn, I saw a black model-T Ford parked just outside our dooryard.

"Rob, that's *his* car," said Soup.

"You mean Mr. Cyrus McGinley's?"

"Yup," said Soup.

"I wonder what he's talking to my mother about."

"It ain't about trout fishing."

"Maybe I best not go home," I said. "At least not until the kettle simmers down."

Soup nodded. "Only a blind fool walks into a hornet's nest and kicks up a dance."

"Hey, does Mr. McGinley know us?"

"Most folks do," said Soup with a sigh.

"Do you think it's about the barn we painted?"

"*You* painted it," said Soup.

"But *your* name's on it."

"That," said Soup, "is my very next problem."

Soup and I walked a few cautious steps closer to our house. Everything was still. We couldn't hear any voices, and Mr. Cyrus McGinley had a voice that, when he was angry, would travel at least a mile upwind.

"Things are sort of quiet, Soup."

"Not for long."

"Hey! Somebody's coming out the door."

"Who is it?"

I smiled. "It's your mother."

"Ma? I wonder what *she's* doing."

"Visiting *my* ma and Aunt Carrie."

"I don't like it," said Soup. "Do you?"

"Well," I said, "I'm not exactly joyful."

Soup sighed. "I'm sure glad."

"About what?"

"I'm glad *I* didn't paint McGinley's barn."

"But it was your idea, Soup."

"Yeah, and now we need another, and fast. Painting my name on his dumb old barn was *my* brainstorm. Now it's *your* turn for an idea."

"Maybe we could run away."

"Not now we can't."

"Why not?" I asked Soup.

"My mother just spotted us. Here she comes."

"Why is she walking so fast?"

"All mothers do that," said Soup. "It's when they're dying to find out if you've done something. Especially if they already *know* you done it. They always walk fast."

"And your ma walks faster than most folks run."

"Luther!" yelled Mrs. Vinson.

"Hi, Mom," said Soup.

"Howdy, Mrs. Vinson," I said. She didn't answer.

"Luther, I want an answer from you, and I want it straight out."

"Yes'm."

"Mr. McGinley is inside. I was here when he pulled his car off the roadway in a cloud of dust and told Mrs. Peck and me about the red paint."

"What red paint?" asked Soup.

"Robert!" My mother was now outside and calling to me from the front veranda, and I could tell by the sound of her voice that she, too, wanted to ask me a question about red paint and barns and ladders. It was good, I suddenly remembered, that we'd gone to Soup's house after I painted the barn, so that we could clean off my clothes (and body) with turpentine. I still smarted from the stuff.

"You know very well what red paint," said Mrs. Vinson. "Did *you* paint Mr. McGinley's barn?"

"No," said Soup.

"You *didn't?*"

"Not one drop," said Soup.

"Come here, Robert!" My mother waved.

I couldn't decide whether to stay and listen to Soup fib or go talk to my mother and fib for myself. Sure was a tribulation.

Soup's mother said, "Mr. McGinley said that someone wrote SOUF on his barn."

"My name's Luther," said Soup.

"Your name is going to be *mud,*" said Mrs. Vinson, "if I find out that you had *anything* to do with Mr. McGinley's barn."

"Anything?" Soup looked troubled.

"Robert," my mother called again, "if you don't get over here this instant . . ."

"Luther," said Soup's mother, "we are going inside to talk to Mr. McGinley."

"Now?"

"Yes, right now. He has some questions to ask both of you."

"About his barn?" I asked. That old funny feeling was in my stomach, a sensation telling me that I didn't want to eat any supper.

"Whatever you do," whispered Soup, as the pair of us (Mrs. Vinson bringing up the rear) marched toward my mother, my house, Mr. Cyrus McGinley, and certain death, "whatever else you do, don't throw up."

"I'll try," I told Soup.

"What are you boys whispering about?" my mother asked us, as soon as the five of us met on the veranda.

"Digestion," said Soup.

Mr. Cyrus McGinley was tall and thin as a dryspell bean. He had long arms and big hands, and a nose sharp enough to pry a lid off a paint can. His head was bald, except over his ears where wisps of gray hair sprouted like two tufts of late-autumn milkweed. He sure as certain wasn't smiling. Cyrus McGinley had a face that would scare a skunk.

"Them's the two," he said, pointing a scrawny finger at Soup and then at me.

"Are you sure?" asked Mama.

"I seen them two up and around my place more'n once, I can tell ya, nosing around and smelling out mischief. Trouble-breeders."

"About your barn . . ." said Mrs. Vinson.

"Some dang fool," said Mr. McGinley in swelling tones, "painted SOUF on the side of my cowbarn. In red paint. And when I catch the idiot responsible, I'm going to paint *him* red, frump to fetlock."

Soup swallowed. Caught for sure, the two of us were really in for it now. There was blood in Mr. McGinley's eye and he was out for revenge. I had to think of something fast. My desperate thoughts were disturbed by Mr. McGinley's next remark:

"They even painted the manure."

"Well," said Mama, "I'm sure . . ."

"Nuts that do things like that," said Mr. McGinley, "ought to be tossed in the hoosegow and throw away the key."

"Mr. McGinley," said Soup, "do you mind if Rob and I ask you a question, sir?"

"Ask *me* a question? I didn't come here to answer a lot of tomfool questions. I come out to *ask*."

"Just one question," said Soup.

"Well?"

"Are you going to vote for our new football?"

The red paint that I had used to deface Mr. McGinley's barn had been a vivid red. But now his face was turning even redder.

"Football?" He almost shrieked.

"For the school," I said.

"Yes," said Soup, "we want to thank you for your support of the athletic program. That's what Miss Boland calls it."

"Boland? Who the devil is *she*?"

"Miss Boland's the County Nurse," I said, "and she's going to help us get the six boards."

"What six boards?"

"For an *H* at either end," said Soup.

Removing his rimless glasses, Mr. McGinley slowly mopped his dour face with a red bandana, which was no redder than his rapidly reddening cheeks.

"We want to say thank you, Mr. McGinley," I said,

as quickly as my tongue would travel, "for helping our school get the five dollars. Even though we don't have it yet."

"Do you know how to put up an *H?*" asked Soup.

"Put up a *what?*"

Soup answered: "Put up an *H* with a board."

"School Board?"

Idea! I suddenly realized why Mr. McGinley hollered so much when he talked. *The old gentleman was as deaf as a goal post.* Wow! That's it! The only thing that can possibly save Soup and me from total destruction.

"Yes, sir," I said, "the school boards from Mr. Ross Drinkwine's lumber yard."

Soup caught on. I knew he would and he did. It was as if I had hiked the football in the dark and somehow Soup had managed to catch it. And good old Soup, in trouble though we were, would keep the ball hiking.

"Mr. Drinkwine's on the School Board, too, isn't he, Mr. McGinley?"

"Tarnation! What's all this to do with my . . ."

"We just want to thank you," said Soup.

"From the bottom of our hearts," I added.

"And," said Soup, "from the big bottom of Miss Boland's heart."

"Boland?"

"Yes," I said, "and Miss Kelly's."

"Miss Kelly's what?"

"Heart," I said, placing my hand over my own, just

as we always did every morning in school when we pledged our allegiance to the flag. Soup saw me do it, adding to the confusion by placing his hand over *his* heart. He winked at me. Not a full shut-eye wink. More of a flinch that only I could detect. A signal.

"We pledge allegiance," we both recited as though thoroughly rehearsed, "to the flag ... of the United States of America. And to the Republic for which it stands, one nation, indivisible, with liberty and justice for all."

Soup and I dropped our hands down from our now unprotected hearts. And to make the moment even more moving, Aunt Carrie came out on the porch and applauded our pledge of allegiance. She always clapped for anything patriotic.

Soup and I clapped, too.

"What is this place?" cried Mr. McGinley. "Am I in some sort of a loony bin? You're all *insane*. Every doggone one of ya."

"We are not," said Mama.

"Certainly not," chimed Mrs. Vinson.

"Always respect the flag," said Aunt Carrie, a bit on the deaf side herself, placing her hand over *her* heart.

"Let me out of this place," hollered Mr. McGinley, "before I come down with it, whatever it is that ails you people."

Slamming his straw hat on his head, Mr. McGinley ran for his Model T Ford, started it, and then stalled it.

Soup and I followed him outside to wave a so-long. He tried again. The engine coughed but wouldn't start.

"You flooded it," said Soup.

Mr. McGinley sat behind the wheel, waiting, as you're supposed to do whenever you "flood it," wiping his face with a bandana. Soup and I stood alongside, silently watching and smiling, again placing our hands over our hearts.

"Boys," said McGinley, "tell me just one thing."

"Sure," we said. "Just ask, Mr. McGinley."

He asked. "What the heck is a SOUF?"

8

"I saw it," said Miss Kelly.

"You did?" I asked her.

"Yes, I certainly did. Miss Boland came for lunch on Sunday, and in the afternoon, we took a drive in her car."

Miss Kelly had asked me to stay after school. I knew she wasn't mad or anything like that. It was sunny, so Miss Kelly and I walked out behind the school. Some of the red and gold leaves had come down and our feet rustled through a fallen October. We sat on a jigsaw fence of long gray rails and talked. She brought up the subject of paint.

"We did it," I said. "Soup and I."

"As soon as I saw that paint on Mr. McGinley's barn, I remembered the red I had seen on your hands. So I put one and one together and concluded that you and

Luther had tested your hand at exterior decoration."

We sat near a buckeye tree. Bending down, I shucked the spines off a split-open shell and shined the buckeye nut by rubbing it alongside my nose.

"What are you going to do, Miss Kelly?"

"Robert, I'm not quite sure the question you just asked is the main issue. I believe the situation can best be mended by my asking you. What do you and Soup intend to do?"

"I believe we ought to go face Mr. McGinley and tell him that Soup and I were the ones who put red paint on his barn."

"Is that all?"

"Well, I don't guess we ought to stop short of making it right."

"How will you do that?"

"Best we scrape off the paint."

"That," said Miss Kelly, "is what I hoped to hear."

"Soup feels the same way. Actually it wasn't Soup's fault as much as mine. He didn't paint the barn. I did."

Miss Kelly lifted her eyebrows. "So you're saying the whole idea was yours?"

"Not exactly."

"I thought not. Having observed one Luther Vinson for several years, I would conclude that he had a hand in everything . . . except the paint."

"Seeing as I put the paint up, maybe old Soup ought to take it down, while I lie under a tree and eat a Jonathan."

"Best apple there is," said Miss Kelly.

"Uh, did Miss Boland see the barn, too?"

"Come now, Robert. One would have to be blind-folded *not* to see it."

"What did Miss Boland say?"

"I can't repeat her exact words," said Miss Kelly. "But I was there when she stopped the car to crank down the window so that we could both take a better look."

"We painted the barn so Soup would win."

"So I presumed. Miss Boland and I both laughed, tears rolling down our faces, until we suddenly became aware of *who* owns the barn."

"Mr. Cyrus McGinley," I said.

"Indeed he does."

"Maybe he doesn't understand politics."

"Do you?"

"Yes," I said. "Campaign managers do all the work."

Miss Kelly smiled. "Incidentally," she said, "the poster you made, an adaptation of Mr. Kapuso, was very amusing. And creative."

"Do you think we picked up any votes?"

"Well, now," said Miss Kelly, twisting the stem of a yellow maple leaf in her fingers so that the hand of the leaf spun round and round in an autumn waltz, "I would predict at this very moment that the election is going to be a close tally."

"Because our school is half boys and half girls?"

Miss Kelly nodded.

"Do you think all the boys will vote for Soup?" I

asked Miss Kelly. "Or will some vote for Norma Jean?"

"Well," she answered, "I believe I could name *one* boy who'd like to vote twice."

"You mean *me?*"

"I do."

"By the way, I'm sure glad you didn't make me read that note in school, the note that Norma Jean Bissell wrote me."

"Looking back," said Miss Kelly, "I am rather ashamed of myself for even *asking* you to read it aloud. Teachers make mistakes, too, you know."

"They *do?*"

"Certainly we do. I saw you reading her letter instead of your geography book. So temper took hold of me."

"You didn't *look* real mad."

"An inner temper. So, in that one moment of haste, I ordered you to read a letter. Something I should not have done, as it was personal. And when you chose the ruler, as opposed to reading the letter aloud, you made me feel more than a little ashamed."

"Honest?"

"Honest and truly." Miss Kelly tapped the top of my head with the leaf. "In spite of my being petty and vengeful, *you* were noble. You acted with honor."

"Sort of like Ivanhoe?"

"Yes, very much like Ivanhoe."

"But he had a horse and a sword." I picked up a stick and began to jab away at an imaginary enemy.

"As you mature, Robert, you will learn that being

honorable is far more shining than either a sword or a horse."

"You're right about all that."

Miss Kelly smiled. "How rewarding it is to learn that, upon occasion, I am right about *something*."

"I didn't mean it like that."

"No, you didn't."

"It just sort of . . . popped out."

Miss Kelly nodded. "In the same way I popped out my order to you to read Norma Jean's note. I apologize for that."

"You don't have to apologize. I started it."

"I wanted to tell you that I was sorry," said Miss Kelly, "just to put things right once again. Did you ever do something wrong, and want to undo it?"

"You mean like painting the barn?"

"Yes. Like the barn."

"Me an' Soup'll fix it."

"Soup and . . ."

"*I* will fix it," I smiled.

"If you're going to answer Norma Jean's letter, best you use A-number-one English."

"I tried a few times. But everything I say sounds sort of . . ."

"Mushy?"

I nodded. "Inside me, there's all these feelings that I have for people. Like the way I feel about Soup and our cat and about Norma Jean."

"I have a possible idea."

"You do?"

"Try writing a *poem* for Norma Jean."

"You mean . . . like Lord Byron?"

"Or like Ivanhoe."

"I want Norma Jean Bissell to be my girl. Sometimes it's all I can think about, even when I should be thinking about Tibet or Manitoba or someplace like that. Even when I help Pa with the milking, I can close my eyes, lean my head against a cow, and see Norma Jean's face. Way down in the milkpail."

Miss Kelly smiled. "When a lad envisions his girl's face down inside a pail of milk, it surely must be love."

"How do I *tell* her?"

"Perhaps in poetry. Boys, you see, don't understand girls. And even grown men fail to understand women. Oftentimes, boys—even big boys—think that what impresses a girl is muscle."

"What *does* impress a girl?"

"Poetry and music. Most of all, courting."

"Courting?"

"Yes. Many a girl's heart has been won, not by the biggest or the strongest or even the most handsome, but by the chap who knows how to court a queen."

"Sort of like Sir Walter Raleigh."

"Exactly."

"I'm not very good at courting."

"How much have you done?"

"Not very much. I gave Norma Jean a daisy once. Is that courting?"

"Indeed, it is. *One* daisy can possibly be prouder than a whole bouquet. What did she do with the daisy? Did she wear it in her hair?"

"No," I said. "She pulled off the petals."

Miss Kelly sighed. "That's because it takes as much practice to become a princess as it does to become a knight."

"Miss Kelly . . ."

"Yes?"

"Suppose you were talking to Norma Jean right now, instead of me."

"And?"

"What advice would you give *her*?" I asked.

Miss Kelly softly folded her hands on her lap and looked upward into the orange leaves. "Well, I believe I would tell her this: Never give your heart to a boy unless, in one way or another, he sings beneath your window."

"I don't guess I sing very good."

"Very *well*."

"Okay, I don't sing very well."

"That, dear Robert, has little to do with love."

"Maybe I should take up the fiddle."

"Perhaps. But let me tell you this. Inside your heart, a violin already plays, for love is a sweet lyric all it's own."

"Never," I said. "I'll never be able to look Norma Jean Bissell right in the eye and tell her my feelings."

"Lord Byron would."

"Ivanhoe would?"

"Most surely he would. In a thrice Ivanhoe would sheath his sword, dismount from his charger, and sing beneath the yellow window of fair Lady Rowena."

"I think Ivanhoe had it easier."

"How so?"

"Well, maybe Lady Rowena is a lot easier to court than Norma Jean Bissell."

Tossing back her head, Miss Kelly laughed a little laugh, then stretched forward her hand to muss up my hair. Which was already mussed up from football with Janice. Miss Kelly pulled a burr off the back of my sweater. Eyes twinkling, she threw me a wink.

"Give your girl more poems than promises."

"And," I said, "sing beneath her window. When do you think I should do that?"

"After," said Miss Kelly, "you scrape the barn."

9

"I'll carry the top," said Soup.

"Okay," I said, "I'll carry the bottom."

The sun was just coming up that Saturday morning when Soup and I sneaked into his Uncle Charlie's barn. Inside, it was still night, but as soon as our eyes adjusted to the darkness, we found what we went for. As we fetched the ladder quietly out of the barn, I noticed why Soup always liked to tote the top of the apple ladder. Up there, the rungs were shorter and lighter. Good old Soup.

"Let's take a short cut," whispered Soup.

"Across the brook?"

"Yeah, and then up over the ridge. I figured we can get this ladder to Mr. McGinley's barn in ten minutes, providing."

"Providing what?"

"We cut across Tinker's pasture."

"No." I stopped walking. "Mama said I was never to cut crosslots through Mrs. Tinker's meadow. Not in the dead of night or in the dead of winter. Not ever."

"I'm not afraid," said Soup.

"You will be if you see him."

"We probable won't."

"How do you know for sure?" I asked Soup.

"Just a hunch."

"Well, if you want *my* opinion of this whole business," I told Soup, "best we don't cut crosslots anywhere near the Tinker place."

Lugging the ladder, we crossed the brook, Soup first. He kept his sneakers dry by stepping really careful on the stones. Both my feet got soaked. Then uphill, Soup at the top of the ladder while I brought up the bottom. Once over the ridge, we could see Mr. McGinley's barn, just the yonder side of Mrs. Tinker's property.

"Hurry," said Soup.

We ran. Our sneakers made dark green footprints on the silver that frosted the short meadow grass. The ladder didn't seem heavy at first, but now that my arms were growing a bit weary, it seemed to weigh a ton. To make matters worse, my hands were starting to sweat; like always whenever I did something that Mama or Aunt Carrie told me I wasn't ever to do. Like cross Mrs. Tinker's pasture.

We saw him. And *he* saw *us!*

"Run," yelled Soup.

Butinski was one heck of a big billy goat. Bigger than a horse. Well, maybe not quite as big as a workhorse, but doggone near as big as a pony. And ten times as mean. People said that old Mrs. Tinker, who was a widow, kept old Butinski on the run-loose, on account she didn't cotton to kids running crosslots through her property.

"Faster," hollered Soup.

"Is he coming?" I was panting so hard that I could barely fire out the question.

"He ain't exactly retreating."

He sure wasn't. Looking over my shoulder, I saw Butinski headed our way at a full trot. And *he* wasn't carrying a ladder. That was when I passed Soup. I was still carrying the heavy end, but I pulled up even, and then raced by Soup like he was parked.

"Wait," puffed Soup.

"Wait? I'm not waiting for that billy goat. I heard tell he eats your clothes."

"Not even a starving moth would eat *yours*," panted Soup, more out of breath than I was.

Butinski was gaining, and I was sure bent on his not catching up to *my end* of the ladder. Or my end. When I heard old Butinski let out a snort, which sounded more like a snarl, I figured we were in for it. Ahead lay the far fence and safety, a good hundred yards away. Yet it was no use. Soup and I were tired. Butinski was fresh. And *his* four legs were quicker than our four.

"Run," cried Soup.

Soup and I ran neck and neck, exactly one ladder apart. Between us and the fence was a tall and lonely elm. We would have to pass it enroute to our escape. We passed it. Or rather to say, we almost passed it, as Soup ran on one side of the elm and I chose the other. When you're carrying a ladder and chased by a mean billy goat, a mistake like this can amount to one bad blunder.

Whack!

The middle of the ladder hit the tree, bent, and then threw us both backwards as if we'd run into a pair of diving boards. Suddenly, there we were, running *backwards*. Not really running. Stumbling would be more like it. And here came Butinski, just as Soup and I lost control of the ladder and fell.

If you look right close at a ladder, other than the legs and the rungs, what you'll see is some squares of air. But what Soup and I saw was Butinski's head—and horns—stuck through one of the holes, halfway between Soup and me. It could have been the first time that Butinski ever wore a ladder around his neck, and from the way his hoofs were pawing the ground, he wasn't very happy.

"We got him," Soup yelled.

I was trying to get up on my feet and not let go of my end of the ladder, while Soup was busy clinging to *his* end. The ladder, meanwhile, seemed to be holding onto that old billygoat.

"What'll we do?" I hollered.

"I'm thinking," Soup hollered back.

"So is Butinski," I said, "and I think that *he* thinks he doesn't like us very much."

"We got him *now*," said Soup.

"Yeah, and he's got us."

"All we do now," Soup pointed across the meadow, "is to ease our way over to the fence."

"How?"

"Best way we possible can."

Butinski twitched his head from side to side, with a mean expression on his face, his horns rattling along the wood that was holding him prisoner. My stomach felt sort of sloshy.

"Soup . . ."

"Now what?"

"I gotta go to the bathroom."

"At a time like *this?*"

"Right now. Can you hold the ladder?"

"Who'll hold the other end?" Soup asked.

"The goat."

"He'll get loose."

"No, he won't," I said

"Hurry," said Soup.

I hurried, my fingers fumbling with the buttons on my trousers, while Soup was gripping the ladder so hard his knuckles were turning white.

"That goat is getting ornery," said Soup.

Soup was right. Butinski was twitching and butting something fearful. One of his horns came loose. I was so excited that my fingers ripped off a button. I saw it fall to the ground. There it was, a little white face with its four tiny eyes, looking up at me. I sort of stood there, staring down at it, not saying or doing anything. That was when Butinski kicked up his heels and charged my way, ladder and all. Soup hung on like his hands were glued to that ladder.

"What's the trouble?" asked Soup.

"It's a button."

"A *what?*"

"One of the buttons came off my pants."

"Forget it," said Soup.

"I don't dare. Mama said I wasn't to lose any more buttons, and if one came off, I was to always fetch it home so she could sew it back on."

"Then pick it up!"

"I don't want to."

"Why not?"

"Butinski's standing on it."

It was true. As that billy goat's hoofs were dancing around, I saw my button down under harm's way. I didn't have the courage to get any closer.

"I can't get the button," I told Soup.

Butinski let out one heck of a mean-sounding snort as if to tell me that I wasn't ever to get my button back. His hoofs were prancing on it. I was so excited I forgot all about how much I had to go to the bathroom.

"Grab your end of the ladder," said Soup.

"Will you get my button?"

"Okay, I'll try."

"Good," I said.

"Rob, get his attention."

"I think we already got his attention. Now all we need to do is get back my button."

"You and your dang button."

I never knew a button could make a goat so angry. Not that Butinski was getting red in the face, or anything like that, but he sure was bucking around more than a bit. Each time that billy goat kicked up his hoofs, I thought for sure his horns would come untangled and that would surely be the end of us. I didn't even care about the button anymore. Or about going to the bathroom. I just wanted to escape.

"Maybe he's hungry, Soup."

"Great. We'll feed him your stupid button."

With his head still caught in the ladder, Butinski charged at me again with fire in his eyes. It was all I could do to keep my fingers around the bottom rung of the ladder. Soup bent over and was searching for the button.

"I can't find it," yelled Soup.

"It's white," I told him.

"Well, it's gone."

"Jeepers, if I come home without that button my mother will kill me."

"Hang on to that ladder or your mother won't ever have the pleasure."

"Keep looking," I hollered at Soup.

As Soup was bending over, searching wildly through the grass, Butinski saw Soup's behind. Ladder and all, he lunged forward, head down and full speed. A second later, Soup was sort of flying forward, with a real surprised expression on his face. I never knew a goat could laugh, but Butinski sure did. Then I heard another sound, a voice, but it sure wasn't laughing.

"Hey!" yelled Mrs. Tinker.

Turning around, I saw Mrs. Tinker marching our way with a bonnet on her head and a long willow switch in her hand. I wanted to run, but my feet were stuck inside my wet sneakers, which seemed to be nailed to the ground.

"What in tarnation are you boys doing?"

Soup said, "We're looking for a button."

Mrs. Tinker said, "With a *ladder*?"

Folks around town said that Mrs. Tinker was so sour that she was weaned on a pickle. And that she never laughed. Never in my whole life did I ever see anybody chuckle louder than Mrs. Tinker. She laughed so hard, she cried, and then sat down on the pasture grass and laughed some more. She was holding her sides, and then when Butinski laughed again, I though she'd near to bust a rib. Finally she stopped and got hold of her goat. So we took off our ladder and ran.

We never found the button.

10

"Done at last." Soup sighed.

"All the red paint is off the barn."

"The manure's still red."

"Well, it'll just have to stay red. I'm plumb tuckered out. Come on, let's get the ladder back to your Uncle Charlie."

We toted it back.

"Now what'll we do?" I asked Soup.

"Let's jump in the hay. I saw a great place for hay-jumping inside Uncle Charlie's barn."

"I'm too pooped."

"Aw, you're always tired," Soup said.

"That's because I do all of the painting and most of the scraping. All you candidates do is boss."

"Somebody has to be the brains," said Soup.

"Sure," I said with a deadpan face.

"Besides," said Soup, throwing an arm around my neck, "you're the best doggone campaign manager that I ever had in my whole life."

"How many have you had?"

"One," said Soup.

Arms around each other's shoulders, we walked along Halpern's Road, which was on the backside of town. Then we climbed the fence behind Mrs. Semple's seamstress place and cut through the junkyard so we could tightrope across Putt's Crick on the fallen log. We were passing behind the row of houses next to the Baptist church when my head went through the tire.

"Gotcha!" yelled Janice.

It wasn't just an old car tire. Janice Riker had dropped a truck tire off Mr. Backlee's garage roof, and there it was, snug around both Soup and me, like a cowboy would lasso a pair of bull calves. So tightly was the truck tire wedged around Soup and me that our arms were pinned to our sides. Helpless!

"Darn ya, Janice," yelled Soup.

"Please," I cautioned, "don't rile her up."

There was Janice up on Mr. Backlee's two-story garage roof, her mean old face looking down at us and spitting. She missed, lucky for us. But I could sure tell just by the way she was moving her mouth that Janice was trying to work up another gob.

"Let's run," suggested Soup.

So we ran, until Janice grabbed the rope (the other end of which was knotted around the truck tire) and yanked. Over we went, because Soup and I were pounded into that ring of black rubber like a pair of pegs. And it sure isn't a whole lot of fun to fall down in the dust when your hands are pinned to your sides. Soup and I were face to face, so tight together that I could feel the buttons on his shirt digging into my chest.

"I'm coming down," yelled Janice.

Hand under hand, her sneakers gripping the long thick rope, Janice Riker climbed down. All the way from atop Mr. Backlee's roof to where the rope was tied to the truck tire. The trouble was that the tire was standing up, in a rolling position, while Soup and I were lying down. Me on the bottom and Soup on the top. He sure was heavy.

"Soup . . ."

"Yeah?"

"Roll over a bit, will ya?"

Janice smiled. I could stand Janice once in a while, but never when she smiled, because her show of teeth meant only one thing. Happiness for her and pain for somebody else.

"Ya wanna roll over?" asked Janice.

I didn't answer. And neither did Soup. Looking up, I watched silently as Janice's dirty fingers untied the rope that was around the tire, knotted behind Soup's back. The knot wasn't easy to untie, not even for Janice, and I heard her say a naughty word.

Every autumn, during the final days of October and early November, Putt's Crick sort of stopped being a creek and turned into a shallow mudhole. I didn't think Janice would do it, but she did. With a grunt, Janice started to roll the truck tire. I knew it was rolling merrily along because behind Soup's head I saw sky, mud, sky, mud, sky, mud . . .

"Whoa!" said Janice.

The truck tire stopped rolling just before it got to the bank of Putt's Crick. Never would I have believed that Janice Riker would save Soup and me from such a fate, but she did.

"I don't want you guys to die," said Janice, "too fast." Slowly, she rolled us back up the hill for another go.

"We gotta get out of this tire," said Soup.

"Quiet," ordered Janice. "*I'll* do the talking."

"What about?" Soup asked her.

"Voting," said Janice.

We were (all four of us, if you want to count the tire) back on top of the little hill. Inside the tire Soup was again lying on my stomach, and I sure wasn't in much of a mood for conversation. Few folks are, when wedged into a truck tire. Soup and I must have looked like two fingers poked through the hole of a doughnut.

"I want Norma Jean to win," said Janice.

"So do I," Soup said.

"You *do?*" I asked Soup.

His eye shot me a quick wink. Never had Soup or I been able to outfight Janice. But it usually was a lead-pipe cinch to *outsmart* her. Between her ears, all Janice Riker had was suet.

"Remember," Soup whispered into my ear, "that we're a whale of a lot foxier than Janice."

"Oh, yeah?" I whispered back. "Then how come she's out there and we're in here?"

"No talking," said Janice, "or else."

"Or else what?" asked Soup.

"Ya wanna find out?" said Janice, her fists on her hips in a real fighting pose.

"No," I said.

"And now," said Janice, "let's talk about how both of you guys are going to vote for Norma Jean Bissell on Election Day, which is Monday."

"It's on Tuesday," I said.

"Monday!" Janice raised her voice and kicked the tire.

"Ya know, Rob," said Soup, "we plumb forgot."

"Forgot what?"

"We can't vote unless we register."

"Huh?" asked Janice.

"That's right," I said, as I played along, wondering what Soup was up to.

"You guys better vote for Norma Jean."

"We would if we could," I said.

"But we can't," said Soup.

"Ya can't?"

"No," insisted Soup. "We didn't register."

"Register?" asked Janice. "What's *that*?"

Soup lifted an eyebrow. It was a signal, like football, that he wanted to lateral the ball to me, because he was stuck for an answer. And that was when I caught his meaning and really came through like a tin-star trooper.

"Cash register," I said quickly.

"Right!" said Soup.

"I don't get it," said Janice.

"Simple," said Soup. "Before you can vote next Tuesday, you have to write your name on a piece of paper . . ."

"Called a ballot," I said.

"And then you cast your ballot," said Soup.

"Where?" Janice bent down and glowered into our faces.

"You have to go and put your ballot into Mr. Jubert's cash register."

Mr. Agnew Jubert owned the local candy store. He was near to a hundred years old, according to Soup's best guess, and had the personality of a hungry buzzard. Not only that, but he guarded his big gold cash register tighter than a bulldog guards a bone.

"That's right, Janice," I said. "You don't vote unless your name gets put in Mr. Jubert's register."

"And today's the last day," said Soup.

"For what?"

"To register, Janice."

"Or none of us get to vote."

"Yeah, and Norma Jean Bissell will lose," I said.

"And I'll win," Soup grunted.

"You better hurry, Janice, and go register."

"Best I hurry," Janice agreed. "And you two birds better be here when I get back." Dukes up, she shook a fist at Soup's face and at mine. Turning, she raced off in the direction of Mr. Agnew Jubert's candy store.

"Let's get out of this tire," said Soup.

"Okay, but how?"

"Wiggle a bit."

"I can't."

"Rob, are you stuck as tight as I am?"

"Yup."

"We gotta think."

"Janice'll be back," I said, wincing at the idea.

"Like poison ivy," said Soup.

"Our only chance," I said, "is to roll away."

"Right," agreed Soup, "and I know where."

"Where to?"

"Mr. Diskin's junkyard."

"He might be closed. Sometimes on Saturday afternoon, Mr. Diskin closes up early."

"It's a chance we hafta take. So start rocking the tire."

We rocked it. Nothing happened.

"Rock harder," said Soup.

How, I'll never fully understand or really care about, but we started the tire rolling, along the dirt path next to Putt's Crick, toward the general direction of Mr. Diskin's junkyard. It's not easy to get a tire to roll when you're wedged inside it. But it's quite a bit harder to stop it. Around and around went Soup's head, and the expression on his face was nothing short of sheer panic. As for me, I didn't panic much. All I did was scream.

Faster and faster went the truck tire, through Mrs.

Quinn's sagging clothesline. Soup's head was suddenly wearing a pair of pink panties. That was when, rolling even faster, we crashed through a stand of empty milk cans. Clangs and gongs of empty metal ringing in our ears, we rolled on, to only Fate knew where. It must have been through somebody's garden, because between my teeth was a late-blooming yellow chrysanthemum. And in my nose the strong smell of organic fertilizer.

We stopped it. The truck tire mercifully rolled to a halt in a large patch of prickers. The bumps, of which there had been many, had loosened the tire, and so out we crawled, leaving the black ring of rubber behind us.

Somebody yelled. It was Mr. Jubert!

"Stop thief!"

Not many people in town can catch a fullback like Janice, and Mr. Jubert was the only soul I ever saw do it. Tall and lanky, his legs really reached out. Then, out stretched his long arm and collared Janice quicker than you'd boat a hooked sunfish.

"I was only trying to register," croaked Janice, helpless in the grip of Mr. Jubert, who had no intention of letting her go. Especially someone who had the nerve to tamper with his cash box.

It sure was a scene to watch.

Soup and I both laughed as we sat on a bench and, one by one, pulled out the prickers.

11

"Today's the day," said Soup.

"Sure is," I told him.

We were on our way to school on Election Day, the pair of us breaking into a trot every so often, because I don't guess that either Soup or I would want to be late for school. Not on this day of days.

"Landon is a sure winner," said Soup.

"Yeah," I said. "Poor President Roosevelt doesn't stand a chance. Not against a Republican like Alfred M. Landon."

Soup picked up a pebble and threw it into Putt's Pond, where it landed with a *chump*. Rings grew in widening circles.

"Everybody in town is going to vote for Landon," said

Soup, "except for Mr. Jubert who never got married on account that he's a Democrat."

Reaching into the pocket of my knickerbockers, I unfolded a slip of paper upon which I had written the names of some kids in the school. Not all, just a few.

"What's all that?" asked Soup.

"Well," I said, "as your campaign manager, I thought I'd make an estimate of how certain folks in our school are going to vote."

"All the guys'll vote for me," said Soup.

"Not all," I warned him.

"Is that why you put a question mark after Eddy Tacker's name?"

"Yup. Eddy doesn't like you, and *me* he likes even less. Eddy'll vote for Bissell."

"You got Ally and Rolly down too."

"I know it."

"They'll vote for me, won't they?"

"Maybe yes and maybe no."

Soup stopped. So did I. Heads together, we fingered down the list on my yellow paper. Soup's finger pointed at Sue Terwilliger and then at Alice Wilson. "Hey! Both of those *gals* will vote for Norma Jean, won't they?"

"Nope," I said.

"How come?"

"Boy," I said to Soup, "are you dumb. Alice is sort of sweet on you and you don't even know it."

"Sweet on *me*? What gives ya *that* idea?"

"I peeked a look at Alice's penmanship paper."

"So?"

"Instead of ovals," I said, "Alice writes a whole line of nothing but Luther Luther Luther."

"Gee," said Soup, "Alice Wilson? Now I suppose you're going to tell me that Sue Terwilliger is just as sweet on me."

"No way. Sue thinks you and I both smell of cow."

"Reckon we do," said Soup.

"Here's the catch. Sue Terwilliger's hair isn't as blonde as Norma Jean Bissell's."

"That wouldn't bother me," said Soup.

"No, I don't guess it would worry *me* either. But it frets the heck out of Sue Terwilliger. And that, as I got it figured, is why she'll vote for *you*."

"So I'm going to *win!*" said Soup.

No, I wanted to tell Soup, you're probably going to lose. Only by one vote, or two votes on the very outside, but you're going to lose the election, Soup. That was what I wanted to tell him. But seeing as we both had worked so hard to win, I just didn't have the heart. I was too tired for truth.

"Yeah," I said, "you might win."

I wasn't the only boy in school who was sweet on Norma Jean Bissell. For a fact I knew that big old Eddy Tacker thought Norma Jean was sugar candy. And she thought *he* was almost as smart as two gorillas and half as handsome. Ally liked Norma Jean and so did Rolly

McGraw and Jack Sturgis. Would they vote for a *girl?* Maybe so, as I *wanted* to vote for Norma Jean, too. Yet I knew I'd vote for Soup.

"Yeah," said Soup, "as soon as Miss Kelly counts all the votes, and announces that I'm the new president, I'll just walk over and shake hands with Norma Jean Bissell, so she won't feel too grieved."

"Good idea," I told him.

"And then I might even declare a holiday, no school, in honor of my victory."

"You're not the president yet," I said. "And even if you are, Miss Kelly is still the queen, and she's always boss."

"She sure is," said Soup.

"Ya know," I said, "sometimes I sort of hanker that the president of the U.S. of A. was Miss Kelly."

"I'd vote for Miss Kelly for anything," said Soup, "even if it was to be ruler of the whole doggone world, the moon, and half of Saturn."

"Me too."

"In fact," said Soup, "I think that when the ballots are all tallied up, and as soon as I take my oath of office, I'll declare a special *day* sometime soon."

"What kind of a day?"

"We'll call it Miss Kelly Day."

"Like a festival or something."

"Right," said Soup. "I will decree that every kid has to make her a present, and we'll all get to school early and string up Japanese lanterns."

"And some bunting."

"Yeah, and maybe the girls can bake some cupcakes with a *K* on top."

"How come," I asked Soup, "you're so all-fired stuck on Miss Kelly all of the sudden?"

"It ain't all of a sudden," said Soup. Picking up a willow twig, he whacked it against the trunk of a tree as we were taking our last shortcut to the schoolhouse. "I guess that I been thinking all along that Miss Kelly is one heck of a good teacher. And she's a good friend, too."

"She certain is."

"More than that," said Soup, "she's a great lady. She's somebody to believe in."

"You mean like God?"

"Not quite. I can't see God. But I see Miss Kelly almost every day, except for summer. Even then we stop and say howdy and help her feed her chickens. People can believe in her. And I always will."

"Yup, I guess that sums it up," I said.

"There's more to it than that, Rob."

"Like more what?"

"Miss Kelly believes in us."

Soup didn't say any more, nor did he have to, because I knew what he meant about Miss Kelly's believing in us. She had a way of looking at me as if I was the only kid in Vermont, like I was *somebody*, instead of just another farmer's kid who smelled of chores and sweat and cow dung. She could touch me with her eyes. And

I knew that I couldn't ever tell Miss Kelly a lie. To do so would sour my soul.

"She sure can hit you with that ruler," said Soup.

"You're telling me."

"Rob . . ."

"Yeah?"

"When old Miss Kelly whacks your hand with her ruler, do you ever tell your ma about it?"

"No," I said. "Because then I'd get asked what I did to deserve it and I'd probable get another dose to home."

"Same with me," said Soup.

"I sure hate Miss Kelly's ruler," I admitted.

"We'd be rotten kids without it."

"Yeah, we certain would."

*   *   *

We voted.

And as Miss Kelly counted the votes, I watched Soup watch Miss Kelly. Her pencil jotted down a mark for each vote she unfolded from our ballot box (which said Red Cross Shoes on it). Miss Kelly had cut a slit in the lid. We all wanted to crowd around her desk to see but had been told to sit quietly on our benches until the final tally was scored. Soup was holding his breath. He was almost certain to lose, but I was so doggone proud of him that I wanted to lie down on the floor and bawl. Not because he was going to lose, but because I was so lucky to have Luther Wesley Vinson for a pal.

"We have a winner," said Miss Kelly.

I'm going to throw up, I thought. My insides can't take it. My stomach just wasn't cut out to be mixed up in politics. Not even as a campaign manager.

Soup was all smiles. The darn fool! And now the results were going to kick him in the teeth and wreck everything.

"Norma Jean," said Miss Kelly, "you ran a splendid race and we are all pleased with you. But the winner this Election Day is our new president, Luther Vinson."

I couldn't breathe.

"Hooray!" yelled all the kids, except Janice.

Norma Jean even clapped her hands when Soup raised his right hand and took his oath, promising to be a leader strong and true and to always get the rest of the kids to do what was good for the school and for all of us. And then Soup walked over and shook hands, as he predicted he would, with Norma Jean Bissell. Soup didn't kiss her hand or anything dumb like that, but he did bow, sort of the way a bow would have been presented to her by Ivanhoe.

*   *   *

I lay awake that night.

I kept thinking about today, Election Day, and how surprised I had been at the outcome. Somehow my figuring in advance didn't pan out. Yet I was sure how every single solitary kid in the whole room was going to vote, bar none. And I figured, even though I voted for Soup, that Norma Jean was a shoo-in.

"I smell a rat," I said aloud.

Shh! Best I keep quiet or I'll wake up the whole darn family, including the dog. And then Tam will bark until heck won't hold it.

Why can't I sleep? Closing my eyes, I didn't see Soup, because all I saw was the face of another friend of mine. Norma Jean's face. If only I had told her how much I wanted to vote for *her*, as well as for good old Soup. But I had to be loyal, didn't I? Isn't that what knights are supposed to be? I lay awake, wondering if I did right or wrong, and I sort of wished that Miss Kelly would walk into my bedroom so I could ask her if I acted with honor.

The shadows on my ceiling and walls were still, telling no answer, laughing at me because I was only a kid who didn't know the first thing about voting or honor or love. I just kept seeing Norma Jean's face. How broken her heart must be!

I wonder!

Is she lying awake right now, too sad to go to sleep, or too mad? Yet in school she wasn't mad. She even said congratulations to Soup when they shook hands. I saw her lips move. Had the shoe been on the other foot, old Soup would have been crushed to near beyond repair. Losing that election today would have knocked out all his spokes. But that wasn't the answer. How come Soup got elected? Name by name I went over all the kids in the school, all twenty-eight of us.

Then it hit me. Hard!

It took me less than a minute to pull on my pants, shirt, boots, coat, and climb out my window, grab the tree limb, and swing to the ground. Fleet as a doe, I ran across our pasture, passing the Vinson's and then the Rafferty's, stopping only when I got to where I was going. Luckily, there was a moon. Its silvery light sort of washed my face as I looked up at her window.

"Norma Jean," I whispered up, my hands cupping my mouth.

Her face appeared above the sill, looking down at me, and I knew that she also had been awake. Carefully she raised the window, stretching out her hand, much too high for me to ever touch. Or hold.

"It was you, wasn't it?" I asked.

"You know, don't you, Rob?"

"You voted for Soup."

She nodded her head. "You and Soup worked harder for it than I did. Compared to you two, I didn't do anything to get elected. Soup will be a better president. He's the real leader of the school, not me. Soup . . . and you."

I sort of swallowed. "You're not sweet on Soup, are you?"

"You worked so hard for Soup, and you did so much. I just couldn't stand to see *you* lose, Rob. Not after you took the ruler instead of reading my letter."

Something in her voice made me place my hand over

my heart. A whole new feeling, and it wasn't anything like pledging allegiance to the flag. I sort of trembled some.

"Are you cold?" she asked.

"Only on the outside," I said smiling.

Right then, her lips said three words to me, very silently, as though it was some sort of prayer that you say only to somebody in your life who is very special to you and always will be. Had her lips actually kissed me on the cheek, I couldn't have been any merrier. I felt happier than a million bubbles.

Suddenly, I wanted to sing, so I sang. Hand over my heart, I sang beneath Norma Jean Bissell's window. Knowing which song to sing, I thought earlier, would be a problem at a moment like this. Yet it wasn't. I sang the only song of which I knew all four verses:

> *try   thee . . .*
> *My coun-   of*
> *'tis*

Robert Newton Peck writes of the fun and frolic of Vermont farm boyhood, where reason often balances rascality. He also writes musical comedy such as *King of Kazoo*, sings in a barbershop quartet, and plays ragtime piano. Rob Peck visits schools, sometimes even on a horse, to turn kids on to reading, to writing, and to a simple reverence for the land. Born and raised in Vermont, he now lives with his family in Longwood, Florida.